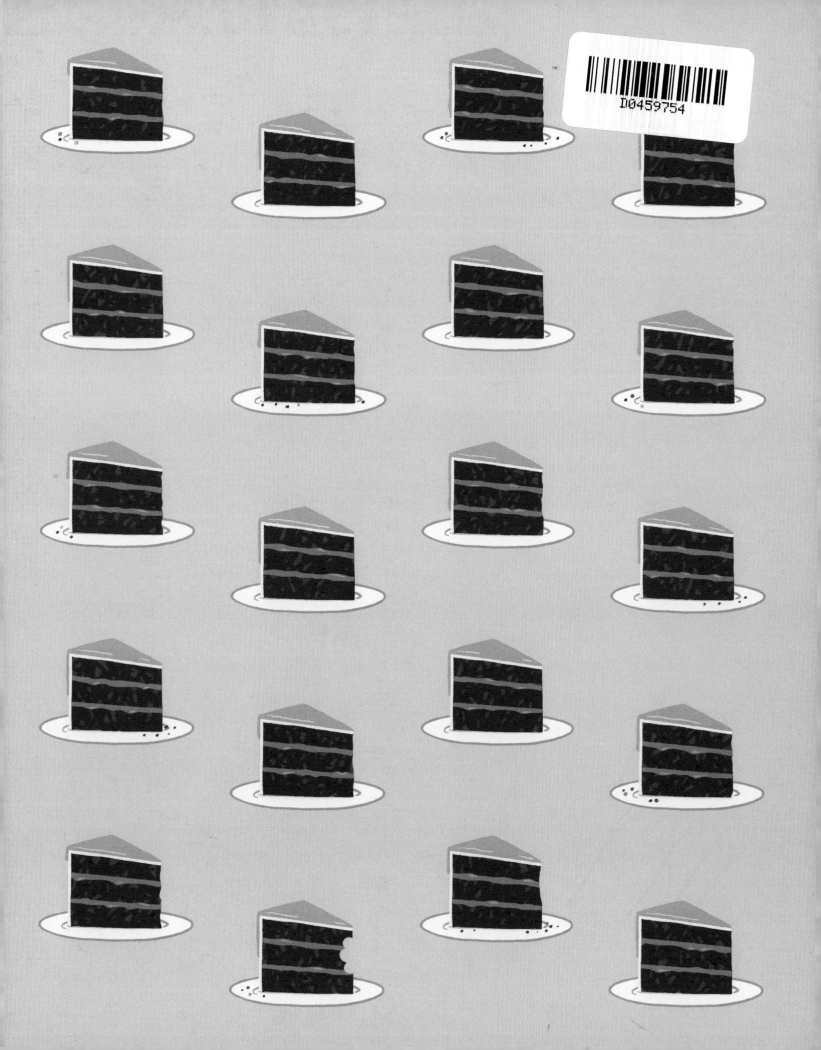

J.C. MᶜKEE
PRESENTS

WITHDRAWN

OH
LOOK,
A CAKE!

CLARION BOOKS | Houghton Mifflin Harcourt | Boston   New York

Oh look, a cake! We should have a party.

Who would you invite?

How about Elephant?

Don't be silly; he'd eat the whole cake.

Tiger?

Oh, she'd eat the whole thing too . . .

And then you. And then me!

Peacock, maybe?

Forget it! That guy won't eat anything
prettier than he is.

What about Ant?

That's just asking for trouble.

Why?

Well, if you invite one ant, you've gotta invite them all. And have you ever tried cutting a cake into that many pieces?

Porcupine?

Only if you like your cake extra spiky.

How about Unicorn? He's so cool!

Wait, what? That's just Horse in disguise.
And, anyway, he's busy today.

There's always Dolphin.

Ha! That showoff would do everything
but eat the cake.

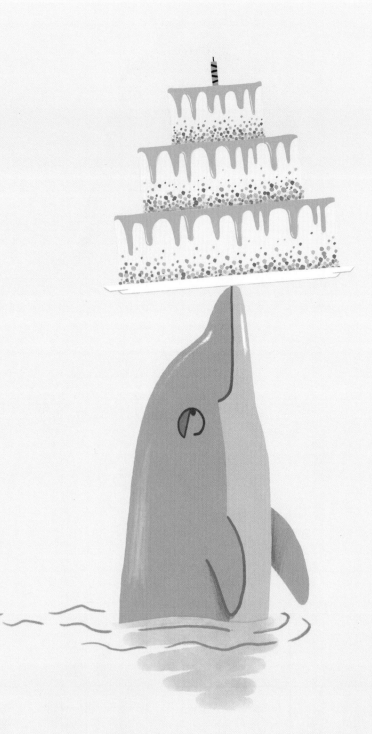

Oh . . . and there's one other thing.

There's no water around here?

Exactly!

Rhino?

She's trouble.

Tortoise?

Sugar does things to him.

Chameleon?

Haven't seen her in weeks.

And Python?

Terrible table manners.

But wait, that means there's no one left
to eat this cake except . . .

Wow.

My cake! You ate my beautiful cake!
That I made! For my birthday!

We're sorry, Tiger!

Oh, don't worry . . .

I can still get it back.

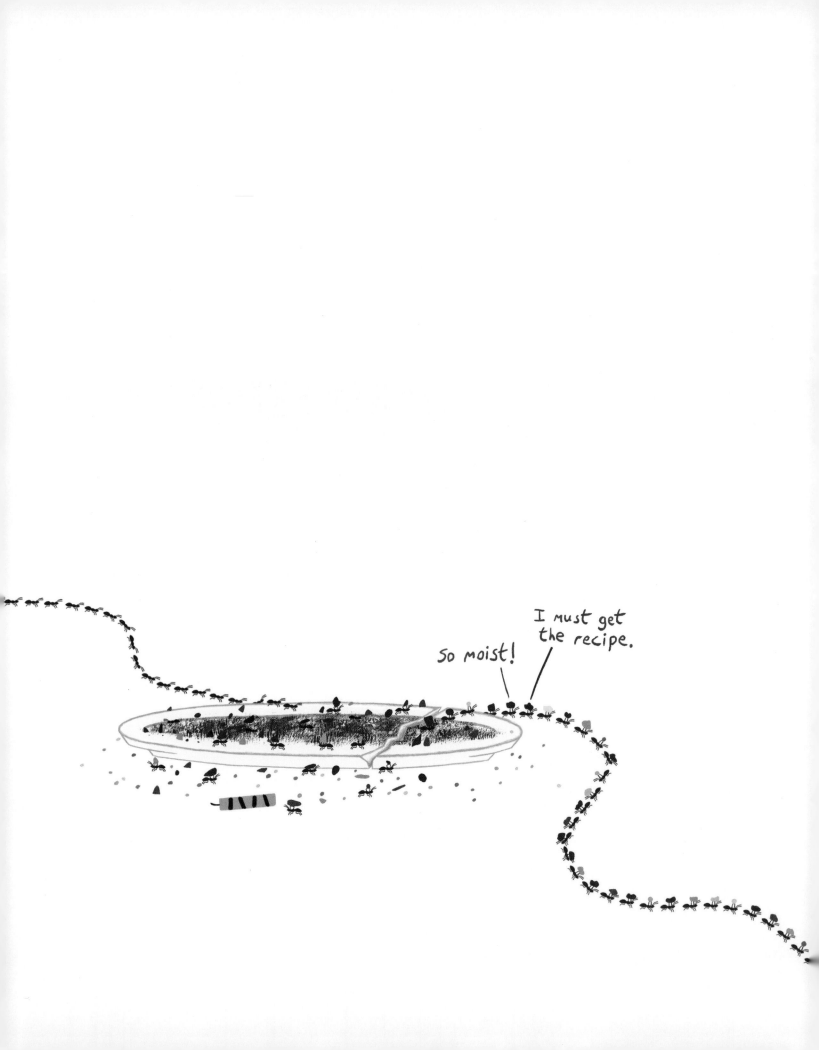

For my grandparents, Eileen and Jim.
Thank you for everything.

Clarion Books
3 Park Avenue
New York, New York 10016

Clarion Books is an imprint of
Houghton Mifflin Harcourt Publishing Company.

hmhbooks.com

No sloths or lemurs were harmed in the making of this book.

The illustrations in this book were done digitally.
The text was set in Fairfield LT Std, National, and Brown Condensed.
Book design by Sharismar Rodriguez

Library of Congress Cataloging-in-Publication Data is available.
ISBN 978-0-358-38030-6

Manufactured in China
SCP 10 9 8 7 6 5 4 3 2 1
4500816938